**For my daughter, Emily,
and all gingernuts**

Copyright © 2000 by Sarah Hayes

First U.S. edition 2000

Library of Congress Cataloging-in-Publication Data

Hayes, Sarah, date.
Lucy Anna and the Finders / Sarah Hayes. – 1st ed.
p.   cm
Summary: A resourceful young girl follows the Finders into the woods near her
house to rescue her little red horse.
ISBN 0-7636-1200-6
[1. Lost and found possessions – Fiction. 2. Resourcefulness – Fiction.] I. Title.
PZ7.H314873 Lu 2000
[E] – dc21   99-089378

2 4 6 8 10 9 7 5 3 1

Printed in Italy

This book was typeset in Cafeteria Black.
The illustrations were done in colored inks.

Candlewick Press
2067 Massachusetts Avenue
Cambridge, Massachusetts 02140

LUCY ANNA
AND THE
FINDERS

Sarah Hayes

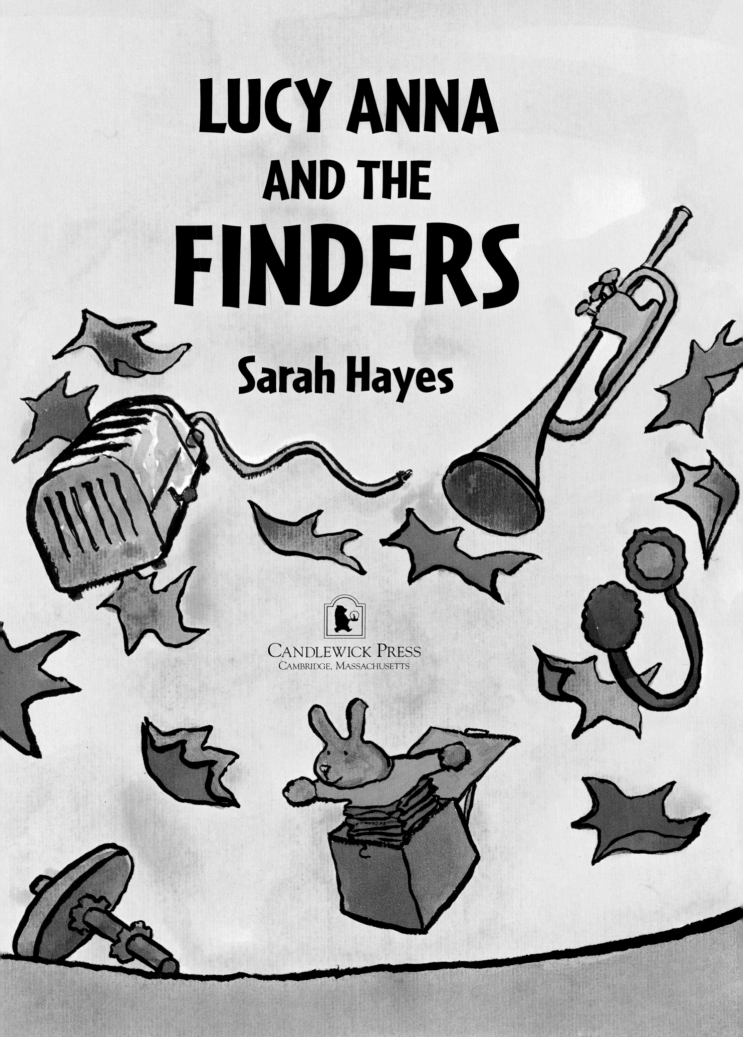

CANDLEWICK PRESS
CAMBRIDGE, MASSACHUSETTS

Not far from the house where
Lucy Anna lived stood a great wood.

And in that wood the Finders lived.

One day the Finders came out of the wood.

They found Lucy Anna's little red horse

and took him away.

Lucy Anna was furious.
She put an apple in her
backpack and marched off
to the wood to get her
little red horse right back.

On her way Lucy Anna
found nine pine cones,
several whirligigs,
and a load of nuts.
She put them
in her backpack.

Then Lucy Anna found

her little red horse.

But . . .

the
Finders
were
there
too.

"I'm taking my little red horse
right back," Lucy Anna said.
"No you're not," said the Finders.
"We found your little red horse
and now we found you.
We're hungry.
We're going to eat you up."

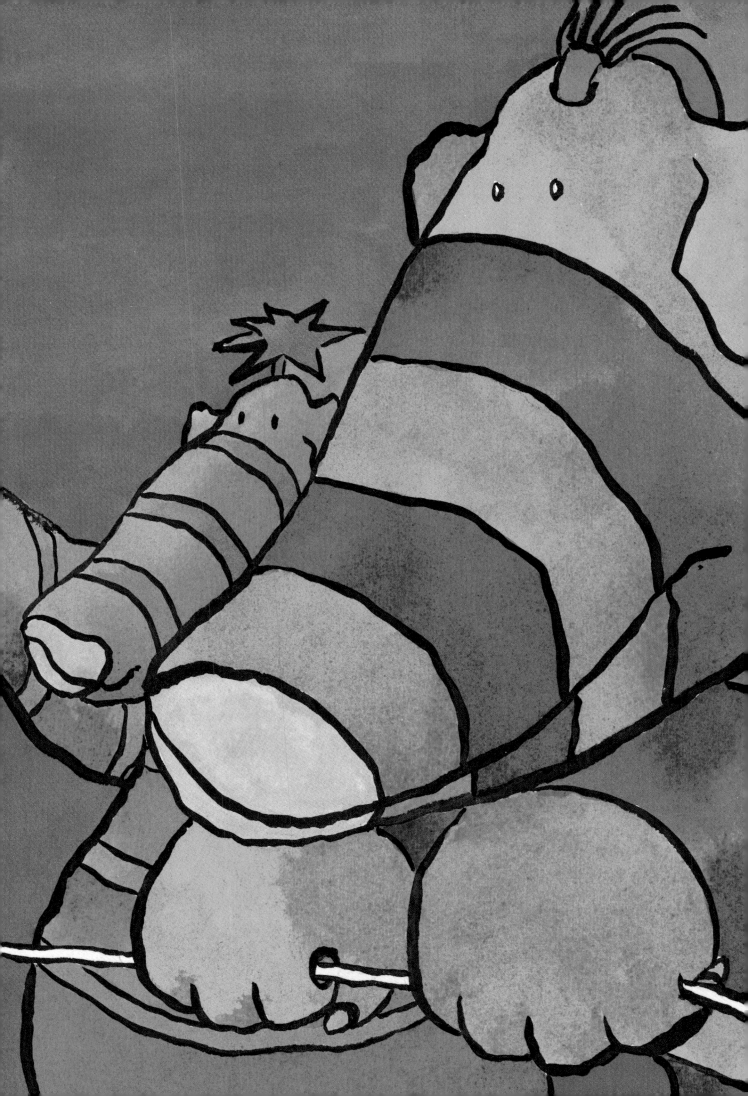

Lucy Anna thought quickly.
She took the pine cones and
the apple out of her backpack
and she began to play ninepins.
"We want to play!" said the Finders.
And they all played ninepins
until the moon came up and
the apple went to mush.

"We're hungry," said the Finders.

"It's not dinner time yet," said Lucy Anna.

And she made a necklace out of a ribbon
and the whirligigs from her backpack.

"We want to try!" said the Finders.

But they were clumsy and
their necklaces fell to bits.

"We're hungry," said the Finders.

Lucy Anna took a nut out of her backpack
and slowly cracked it open.

"We can do that," said the Finders.

But they ate up the nuts
in one crunch, shells and all.

"We're still hungry," said the Finders.

Lucy Anna looked in her backpack and there was **NOTHING LEFT.**

So she ran away and hid.

And the little red horse ran with her.

They hid inside
a hollow tree but the
Finders soon found them.
"We're really hungry now," they said.
"We're going to eat you up right this minute!"
But Lucy Anna had been thinking and thinking.
And now she knew exactly what to do.

"It's my turn to be the Finder,"
she said. "And it's your turn to hide."
The Finders forgot all about
being hungry.
"You'll never find us," they said.

Lucy Anna covered
her eyes and counted.
And when she was sure
the Finders were hiding . . .

Lucy Anna jumped on
her little red horse,
and the little red horse
ran like the wind,
out of the wood and
all the way home.

As for the Finders, they
went on hiding and hiding.
And no one
ever found them.